For Virginia herself, for Amber (because),
and for every child with a dream.—B.K.

I wish to thank the University of Pennsylvania
and the Bassini Writing Apprenticeship,
which supported my research for this book, and, of course,
Amber Auslander, my brilliant Bassini apprentice
who makes her own spectacular new things.

For Micheline,
of the little green house with the raspberry door.—J.B.

Text copyright © 2022 Beth Kephart
Illustrations copyright © 2022 Julia Breckenreid

Book design by Melissa Nelson Greenberg

Published in 2022 by Cameron + Company, a division of ABRAMS. All rights reserved
No portion of this book may be reproduced, stored in a retrieval system, or transmitted in any form or by any means,
mechanical, electronic, photocopying, recording, or otherwise, without written permission from the publisher.

Library of Congress Cataloging-in-Publication Data available.
ISBN: 978-1-951836-38-2

Printed in China

10 9 8 7 6 5 4 3 2 1

Cameron Kids is an imprint of Cameron + Company

Cameron + Company
Petaluma, California
www.cameronbooks.com

a room of your own

A STORY INSPIRED BY VIRGINIA WOOLF'S FAMOUS ESSAY

BY BETH KEPHART

ILLUSTRATED BY JULIA BRECKENREID

cameron kids

Through the jam and cram
of her house she goes.
Through the kitchen.
Up the steps, into the garden, onto the path.

The sky is steel, but there will be blue.
The rooks are quiet, but soon they'll swoon.
And on and on and on she goes,
to that room she calls her own.

Here it is:

Her place to **think**.

Her place to **dream**.

Her place to **be**.

And you?

Where do you go
to **think**,
to **dream**,
to **be**?

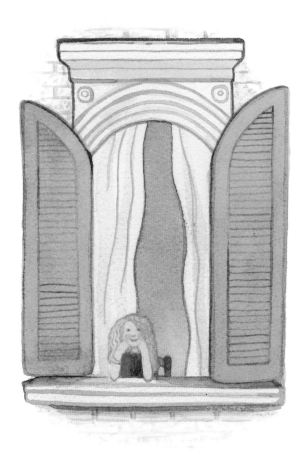

Is the room you love best
small or big?
Is it a glorious mess
or whistle clean?
Does it have walls?
Does it need a roof?
Your room is your room—
it can be anything.

Is the shade beneath a tree
the room of your own—

or is it the stream of sun
dazzling in
beside the nest,
between the leaves?

Is it the cool step
        of a city stoop—
        near the jump rope's swish
        and the sidewalk talk—

or is it the spill of a sill
          with a view,
          or the back of a bus,
          as it zooms by?

LITERARY FICTION

Is the rug on the floor of the store your room—
    all those books
    and all those tales
    just within reach,
    just for you?

Is the corner of the kitchen table
your very own?

Or is your room the cool
    beside the tail of the cat,
    behind the tablecloth,
    where nobody has found you yet?

Or the private dream
inside the night's deep dark?

One needs a room
to be one's
excellent,
imagining,
day-
and night-dreaming
self.

One needs a room
to **think**,
to **dream**,
to **be** . . .

To write.

Virginia Woolf in Her Garden; Rodmell, England, 1926

Photo by Mondadori via Getty Images

AUTHOR'S NOTE

Virginia Woolf (1882–1941) was a British writer of very modern novels—novels that did brand-new things with time and voice and plot. Her books like *Mrs Dalloway*, *To the Lighthouse*, and *Between the Acts* are still widely read today. *How did she write those books?* people wonder. *What were the stories behind her many stories?*

I like to think about the places where her stories came to be. Sometimes it was that chair beside the fireplace. Sometimes her bed. Sometimes the mess of a space plunked down in the midst of a clattering printing press. Sometimes an old garden shed on the edge of her country cottage, and sometimes a fancy room built very specifically for her. By the time she published the long essay "A Room of One's Own" in 1929—an essay in which she famously declared that a woman must have money and a room of her own if she is to write fiction—she had left her mark on many rooms, and they had left their marks on her.

We might not have all the choices she had. We might not have a lock and a key, four walls and a roof, our very own castle, even, but we can imagine our way toward the rooms of our own—the places we'll go to think and to be. Maybe that rocking chair in that cozy corner feels like a place of your own. Maybe the old wagon where you sit and sing is your own spectacular room. Maybe you don't need a private space at all—just a box of color and a sheet of paper.

I wrote this book while lying on my bed. I wrote it while sitting on the couch. I wrote it while riding a train and while standing in the kitchen, stirring the soup with one hand.

Where do you go to think and be, write and dream, create imaginary worlds of your own? I like to think about you, in your own room, making your own spectacular new things.